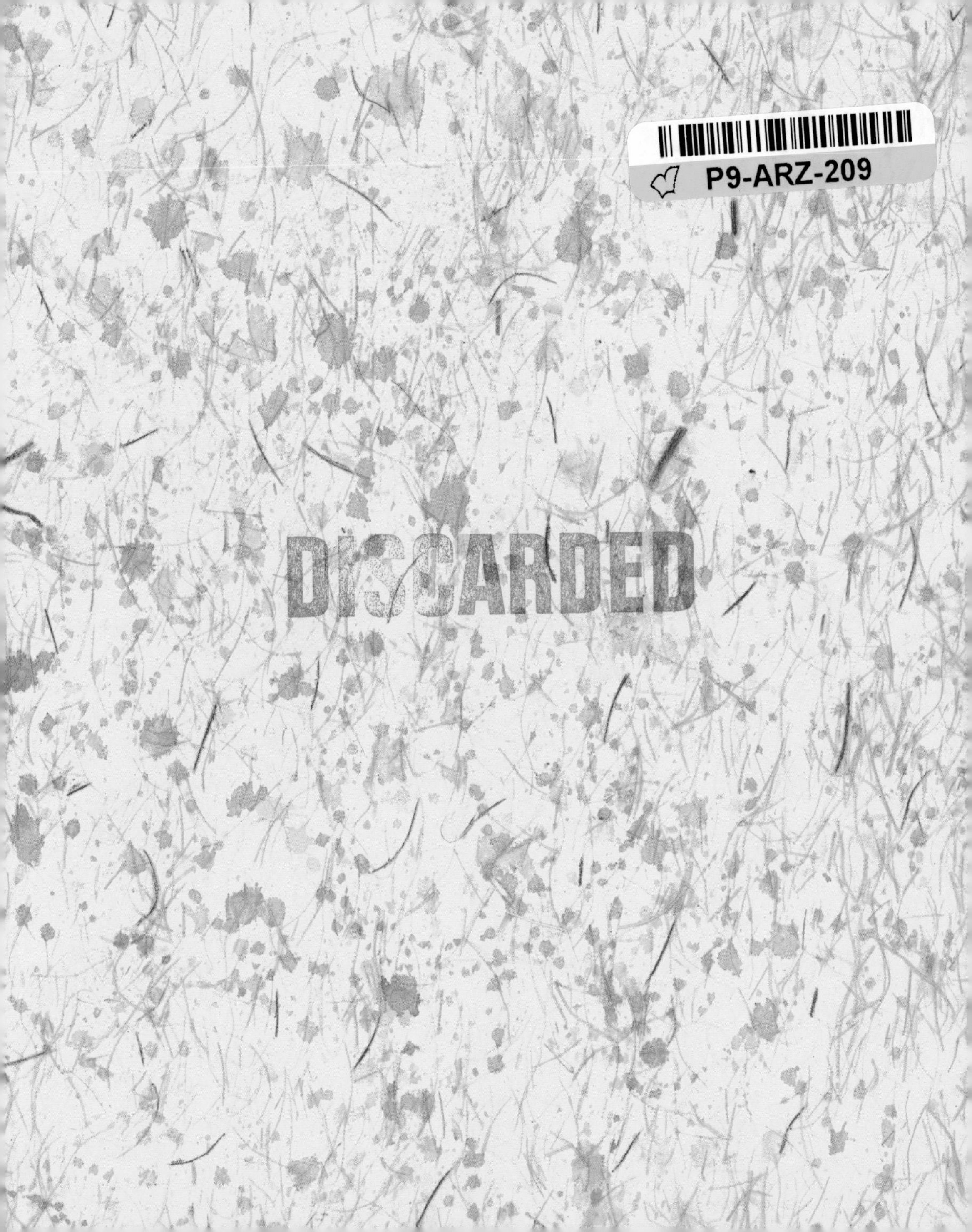

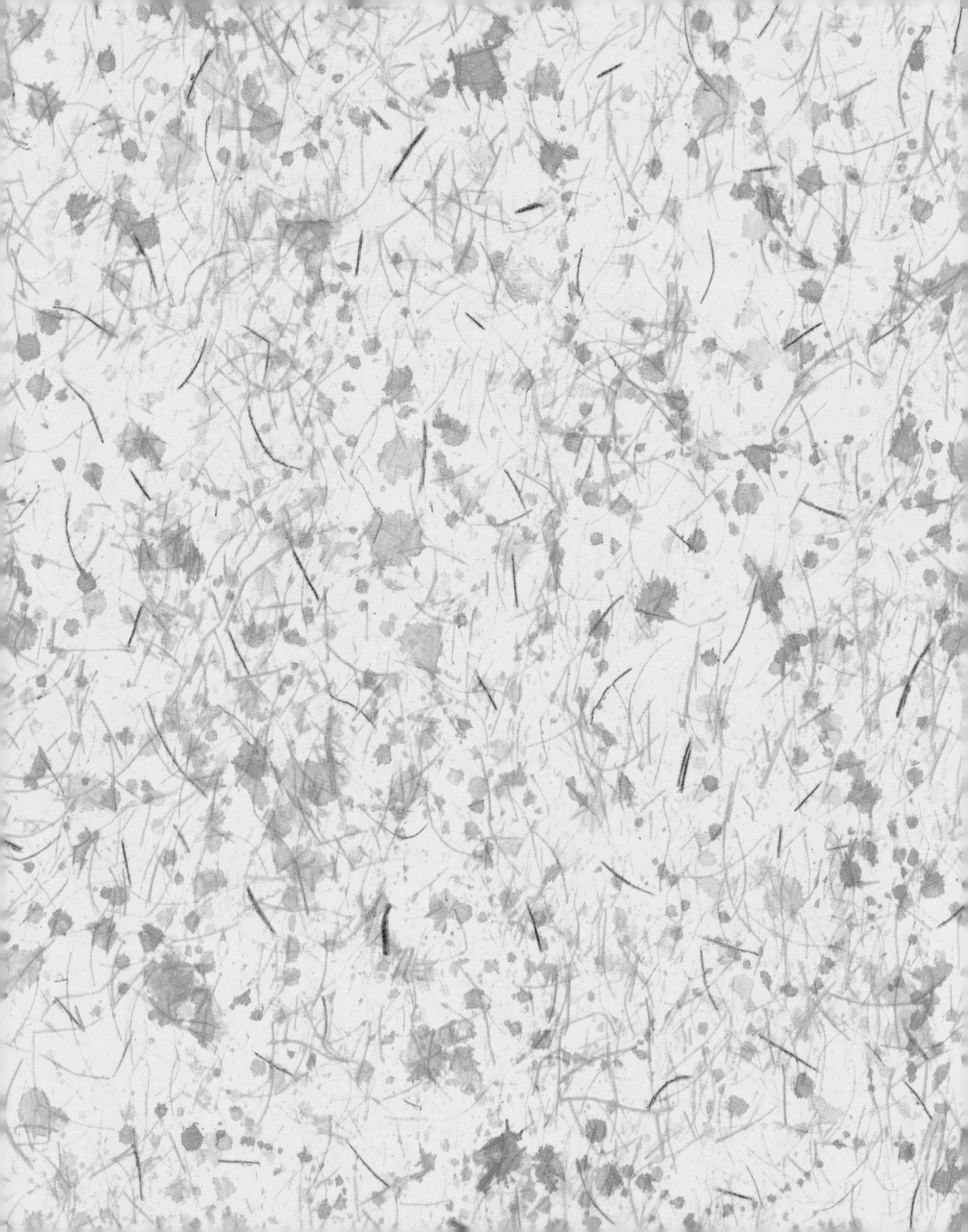

All Alone

KEVIN HENKES

GREENWILLOW BOOKS
An Imprint of HarperCollins*Publishers*

All Alone

Manufactured in China
www.harperchildrens.com

First published in 1981 by Greenwillow Books.
Reissued in 2003 by Greenwillow Books, an imprint of HarperCollins Publishers.

Watercolors and colored pencils were used for the full-color art.
The text type is 24-point Venetian 301.

The Library of Congress cataloged an earlier edition of this book as follows:

Library of Congress Cataloging-in-Publication Data

Henkes, Kevin.
All alone.
Summary: The narrator explains why it is sometimes nice to be alone.
[1. Solitude—Fiction] I. Title.
PZ7.H389Al [E] 81-105 AACR2
ISBN 0-688-00604-3 (trade)
ISBN 0-688-00605-1 (lib. bdg.)

Reissued edition, 2003:
ISBN 0-06-054115-6 (trade)
ISBN 0-06-054116-4 (lib. bdg.)

10 9 8 7 6 5 4 3 2 1

 GREENWILLOW BOOKS

To Mom, for knowing
I should take the chance

Sometimes I like to live alone,
all by myself.

When I'm alone,
I hear more and see more.

I hear the trees breathe in the wind.

I can see through the ground.
The roots make tangled shapes.

I feel the sun's heat all over me.

When I'm alone,
I can change my size any way I like.
I can be tall enough to taste the sky.

And small enough to hide behind a stone.

When it's just me,
I ask myself questions I can't answer.

I think of favorite things I've done.

Then I'm back all alone again.

When I’m alone,
I look at myself inside and out.
No one looks just like me
or thinks just like I do.

I wonder what my friends are doing.

Sometimes I like to live alone,
all by myself,
for just a while.

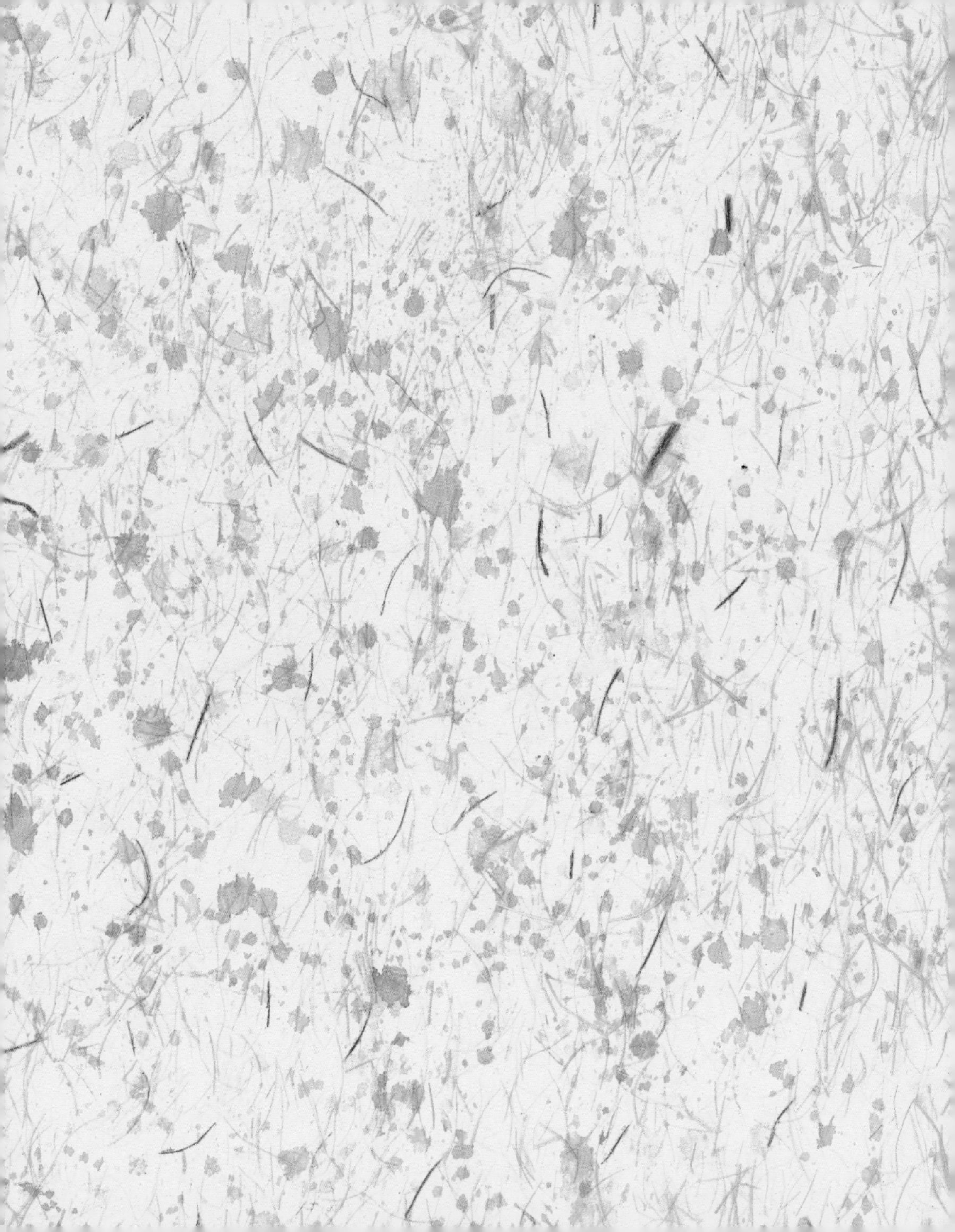

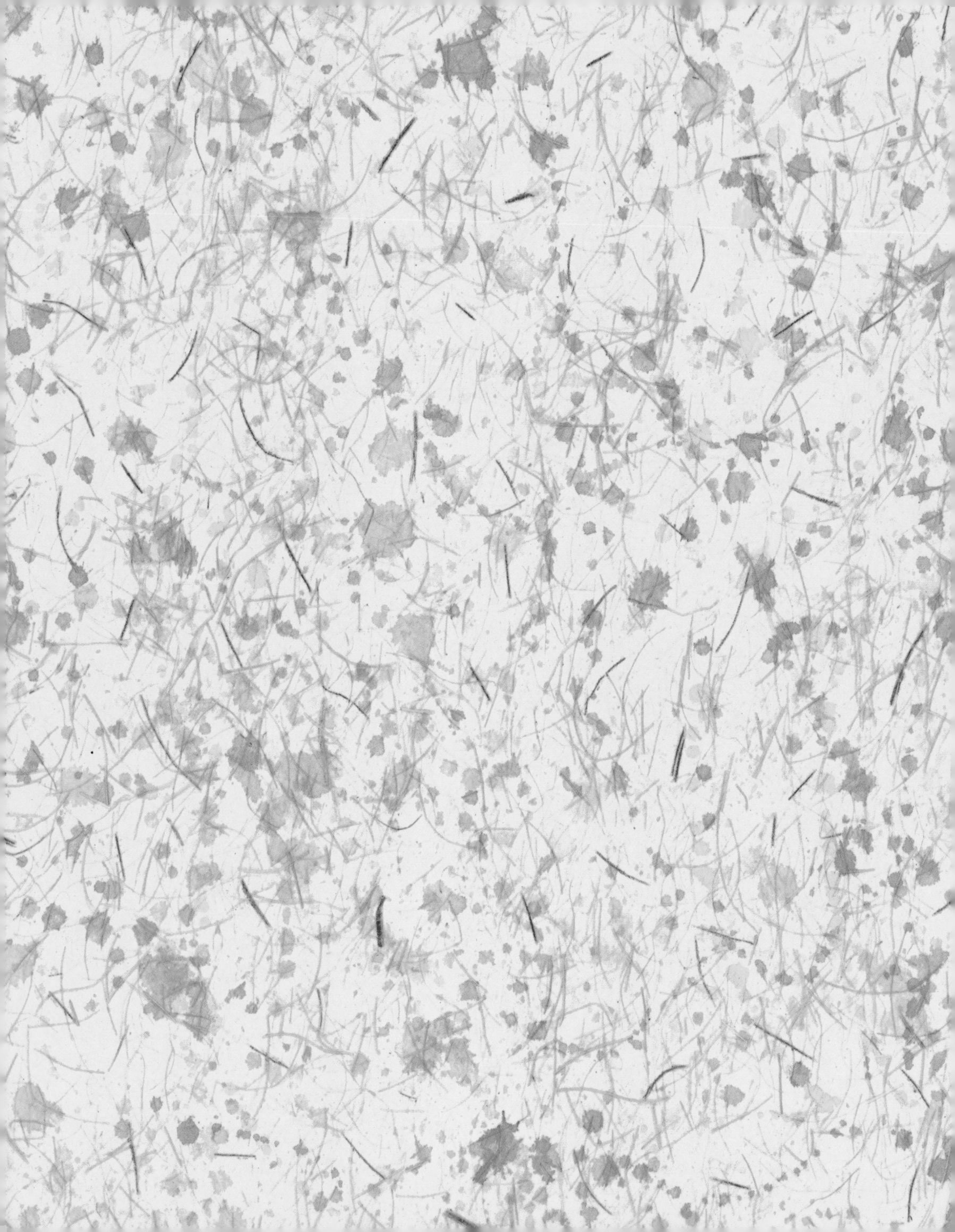